I have been into B.D.S.M., s
and had always wanted to be
transgender Victorian maid of all work. Of course, it was a fantasy, but it is one that filled much of my thoughts to the point where such thoughts dominated my life. So I decided my need was so great to try and find such a position through one of the many B.D.S.M., personal websites. It was a bit of a maze as most subscribers using these websites were only interested in online titillation and not interested in the real thing.

After looking for two years plus I found a possible Mistress who claimed she wanted such a maid in a large manor house near Dover England. She told me the house was occupied by Masters, Mistresses and their slaves who were all in the B.D.S.M lifestyle. If I was to be taken on I would be a housemaid, meaning I wouldn't belong to any Master or Mistress but instead belong to the house and all who occupy it.

The house employs a strict regime of discipline where the housemaid would be micro-managed and will abide by Victorian-style protocols. Mistress told me I ticked all her boxes and I seemed willing to adhere to a protocol of that bygone age, which was employed throughout the house by its entire serving staff.

Below are Mistress's initial emails as she assessed my suitability:

Mistress:

"Yes, I can wait until the 5th although it seems a long way off. What time would you arrive on Friday and need to leave Sunday? If things go well and you pass your first trial when would you be able to be free to stay for a further, longer period of induction?

The problem I have faced so far is turning messages from applicants into firm meetings, hence the urgency I have in finding a suitable maid for our vacant position. There are too few people out there that really want to serve as a slave.

The other reason is those I have seen do not meet my needs and I get very frustrated with this situation. I do prefer a slimmer maid rather than a fatter one, but this can be modified with a strict diet and isn't an important consideration. So if you are a little overweight, don't worry.

I am pleased you came to terms with your status as a slave and fully understand the position I am offering you. You will be a very lowly servant and at the very bottom of the pecking order. You need to realise if I ask you to jump I need to hear you say how high Mistress. If I or any of the Masters and Mistresses approach you when you're doing the ironing or washing up say they need your assistance, you stop what you are doing immediately and attended to my/their needs without any hesitation.

I am not an ogre by any means and am considered by many people I meet in general as being gentle, kind and considerate. All we ask from a slave is just to follow our orders and to do what we ask instantly without hesitation. Notice when I or any of the Masters and Mistresses asks for something it is a command. We will not ask for anything irrelevant or frivolous.

Tell me, slave, do you dress as Daisy 24/7? Do you always go out dressed as Daisy? What limitations do you have in being Daisy currently? I assume when you are going out as Daisy you do not pee in public conveniences, but go before going out and returning home."

Me:

I emailed back and told Mistress I had yet to go out in public and was at the beginning of my transgender experience. The only limitation I was aware of was my voice, but however, no one has said to me it sounded particularly masculine or it was a problem. Whilst I was writing my email I asked a few questions.

Mistress:

"In reply to your questions in your email, you address me as Madam or Mistress at all times. You ask me if I was still working, but I am not, I have opted for early retirement. I spend a lot of time on my computer answering questions from Dommes and Masters. I also get questions from newbie submissives and slaves, and I help them to come to terms with their submissiveness. So I am fairly busy with one thing or another and of course, I am responsible for the domestic staff. I have been in the lifestyle for many years. Three years ago I came into a sizeable inheritance and decided to buy a large house where I along with other Masters and Mistresses could lead a life with other like-minded people. It has worked successfully so far. We achieve this by employing strict discipline.

However, we don't shout at our slaves and maids, we don't need to, shouting is a weakness, our word whether or not spoken softly is a command and will always be obeyed.

For your information maids, fingernails will be kept short at all times and your hair no longer than shoulder length. A simple necklace is permissible along with studs for the ears. One bracelet is allowed providing it will not damage polished surfaces. If accepted for service we will provide a suitable uniform. This will be a knee-length dress, black patent shoes and black stockings or tights."

I wrote back and asked more questions. I did so, so I could get a feel for the position and understand what will be expected from me. This was a serious and life-changing position and I didn't want any surprises and wanted a sense of what life would be like as a Victorian housemaid.

Mistress:

"I do not expect a slave to perfect immediately and appreciate you will need moulding and shaping to fit in with the house's needs. Like many, I imagine it will be a shock to the psyche at first and you'll need adequate time to settle into your new role and do what is expected from you.

Of course, you'll be nothing more than a slave and slaves are not paid, have no rights at all, none, and are here to make our lives easier, you will be completely and utterly selfless in everything you do.

The house will provide all you need to perform your duties. For example, a uniform and rubber gloves will be provided. We will also provide you with a suitable nightie, makeup and manicure set. You will be allowed to keep your outdoor clothing in case you need to leave the house for essential appointments. I will add leaving the house will be extremely rare. You will be accompanied by someone for all such appointments. We will be spending a lot of time and trouble training you, so we won't want you to get lost!

We shall spend a lot of time on female servant-girls deportment. This will involve, naming just a few; serving, sitting, standing and walking. You will be occasionally chastised to keep you the maid submissive and obedient. There will also be a degree of bondage. You'll be employed as a 'maid of all work' but in the future, you may be purchased by a Master or Mistress and your role may change and you could possibly become a lady's maid for example.

Bondage will be used in a few cases often when in the house on your own or as a restraint when being punished. It is needed to gain compliance. But in general, punishment is not used as a routine, but to correct errant behaviour only. I also like to practice Japanese rope work and you'll occasionally be used as my model.

You will be taught to curtsey as you'll curtsey many times in a day, on entering and leaving a room, when addressed by a Master or Mistress to name a few occasions where curtseying is expected by a maid. Your eyes will always be cast down and you'll behave demurely. You will only speak when spoken to.

A maid will eat all her meals in the kitchen. Sometimes you'll be asked to help cook in the kitchen, especially for parties, which we have a few from time to time. At lunchtime, we usually have sandwiches only. You'll have your own room which is a privilege which can be taken away and if that happens, you'll have to make the most of the kitchen floor. If I am charitable I may provide you with a pillow, depending on my mood at the time.

From what you tell me you seem to have a good slave attitude and you're breaking-in period will probably be shorter than some. Of course, a maid works 24/7 and has no days off ever, not even Christmas, unless for compassionate reasons. You will always be encouraged to be feminine and behave femininely at all times."

Me:

I wrote back saying Mistress's terms will be acceptable. I asked two questions and what my duties will be and how would I be punished if my work didn't come up to an expected standard?

Mistress:

"A Victorian maid of 'all work' is up at 6;30 am and is tasked with many duties, ones I can think of in particular is cleaning the fireplaces and grates as we have several open fires in different rooms about the house. As you might imagine, this is a big house covering four floors and a basement. Basically, you'll be tasked with any domestic duties that need doing, you'll be responsible to the head housekeeper who is me and I am, by the way, Mistress Raven. I will also be responsible for any punishment you may require. This is usually administered by me in the basement, which is fairly soundproof. For your interest, I favour a junior dragon cane, which I find always produces good results. You'll not want many visits to the basement that I can assure you.

I suggest to you Daisy to come along for an open day. What I mean by an open day is, that although you'll be expected to dress as a maid, you will not be under any discipline, nor will you be expected to perform any domestic tasks. It will simply be an opportunity for you to meet in a relaxed and friendly atmosphere all the Masters and Mistresses who are present. You will be shown around the house and see all its facilities. If you are good, and I like you, I may also make you up and loan you a maid's dress for the day. You will also meet some of the other slaves and servants and you'll be able to chat with them freely.

If you still at the end of the day want to go ahead and become one of our maids, we can chat about that before you leave."

Chapter Two

I was quite enthused by the Mistress's offer. I liked the idea of going along without any pressure just to see the lie of the land as it were. It would give me a heaven-sent idea of what I might be letting myself in for. There was nothing to lose so I arranged a date to go to the house. Mistress Raven gave me the address and told me to arrive at 9 am sharp and I could stay until about 5 or 6 pm to get a decent feel for the house and its occupants and the work of a maid.

I was so excited I got up early that morning to ensure I arrived on time. I was over an hour early, so sat in the car and waited for 9 am. Sitting in the car for so long wasn't a brilliant idea and although this meeting was to be relaxed I did get quite nervous as I really hadn't any idea of what to expect, I was about to enter the complete unknown.

I didn't get quite the reception I expected as Mistress Raven was annoyed with me for not telephoning and confirming my appointment.

"Never mind you're here now come on in," Mistress said with a touch of annoyance in her voice, but she soon mellowed and was quite good at relaxing me. I was first shown into a large living room where I was greeted by a TG maid and two Mistresses. There was also the Grand Master of the house, walking around in a dressing gown. He reminded me of Noel Coward, as he had all the bearing of someone from the 1920s and was very tall and thin.

I was told to sit and the TG maid brought me a cup of tea, which was most welcome as I was quite parched from the journey. I just sat there and took in the ambience of the place. Mistress Raven was called away and I was just left there to observe all that was going on.

One of the Mistresses was occasionally answering the telephone and I quickly realised the house made its revenue from providing premium B.D.S.M., services. Of course, if I joined them it wouldn't apply to me as I would be virtually 24/7 and providing a real service rather than servicing a fantasy, that's not to say my desire to be a maid isn't based on fantasy.

After about an hour Mistress Raven reappeared with a uniform and frilly petticoat folded over her arm.

"Time to get you dressed Daisy so you'll feel more at home. I have all you need here, so follow me," Mistress Raven said, turning back towards the living room door. I followed her upstairs to her bedroom. I realised there was plenty of money coming into the house, the carpets had a deep pile and everything was tastefully decorated with expensive wallpaper. Mistress's bedroom was huge with an ensuite jacuzzi.

"All the clothes you need are here, as a temporary measure stuff your bra with your socks. Get dressed and I'll be back in ten minutes and we shall have some fun making you up."

I was left on my own to change into the borrowed maid's dress. I confess I felt very titillated when I stripped off and changed into the uniform. The frilly petticoat set the uniform off as it consisted of layers and layers of lace which puffed out the skirt. I resisted the temptation to look in the full-length mirror on the bedroom door. I wanted to wait until I had on makeup and a wig.

Mistress Raven returned and gave me a genuine smile as if she was pleased with my general appearance. She told me to sit at the dressing table and she opened a big case of makeup. I could see dozens of different colour nail polishes and an array of eye shadows just at first glance. Mistress Raven mused over which foundation cream to use. She settled on what I thought, later on, was actually too light for my complexion, but I didn't mind. I was lucky to have all this attention just for me. Mistress must have spent an hour, making me up. I confess I lapped up every second and loved all the fuss she made of me.

The final touch was a wig and then I was left sitting on the end of her bed whilst Mistress Raven fiddled with an expensive camera. Then I was told to stand by the door for a photo. After that, I was taken to the bathroom and I posed as if busy cleaning the shower cubicle. I also had some shots taken on the stairs as Mistress Raven thought I should show off my legs. When the photo session was over I was taken back downstairs and allowed to sit in the lounge and chat. A short while later I was shown around the house which was a lot bigger than I first thought and I thought it to be big, but the house went on forever, room after room corridor after corridor. I can see why they had to offer premium B.D.S.M., services as the house would cost an absolute fortune to run. I could see why they needed domestic slaves to keep the place clean and to keep costs down.

After the tour, I was once again shown back to the living room. The Master of the house saw me for the first time since I was dressed and made up, and he complimented me on how different and feminine I looked. He genuinely seemed stunned at my transformation. I was offered a drink and a sandwich. While I was enjoying these I spoke to one of the maids, a TG who had been in the household for about three months. She told me Mistress Raven was very fair with discipline, but if I ever got on her wrong side I would see a different Mistress. I was told she was very efficient with the cane which was her favourite implement.

Later Mistress Raven showed me the basement, where all physical chastisement was administered. It was the very first time I had seen wooden stocks and spanking benches. There was also a wall lined with every conceivable punishment implement plus a bucket full of different size canes. I also noted two wrought iron cages to keep victims in while they waited to be attended to.

At 5 pm I was asked to change and leave. Before I left Mistress Raven said if I still wanted to be a maid to give her a ring after I had time to think about my day with her. Just as I was going out the door, she kindly gave me a CD with all the photos she had taken during the day. I could wait to get home to see them. There were about twenty high-quality photos in all. I spent hours looking at them. I decided there and then that I wanted to be a housemaid for Mistress Raven.

I left it a couple of days just to be sure this is what I wanted and then excitedly I telephoned Mistress Raven and asked formally if she would consider me as a maid. She seemed pleased and replied:

“We need to take things slowly at first before you’re offered a full-time position. So what I suggest is you come again for another full day, although this time you'll be expected to work and be under discipline. We both want to be absolutely sure that this is what you want. You'll be making a life-changing choice and I want to be sure it is right for you."

I was asked if her proposal was agreeable, to which I replied it was. "Then let's say you come along next week, say on Monday. The Mistress went on to add that a full-time maid would start her duties at 6 am. "However, I realise you have to travel so for your initiation day you can arrive at 8 am prompt and leave at 6 pm. At the end of the day, you'll have a much better idea if this position will suit you for the long term.

I agreed to come along for an initiation day where I will find out what it is like to be a Victorian housemaid. I was so nervous I couldn't get any sleep the night before my initiation. To impress Mistress Raven I arrived early again and waited in the car for the dot of 8 am before going and knocking on the front door of Mistress Raven's house. I think she must have been expecting me as she came to the door almost instantly.

"Hello Daisy," she said, glancing at her watch," You're bang on time, I'm very impressed it is a good start, that is what I like to see, punctuality. Right, come in, come in."Mistress Raven urged and I stepped into the hall. "Well, we can't have you dressed as you are, so do you remember where my bedroom is?" Asked Mistress Raven.

"I think so Mistress Raven," I nervously replied.

"Don't be so nervous, I won't eat you, well not straight away. Off you go and get changed and makeup, take your time, no rush. I know you're not used to making up so just take it slow, you're not on any clock. Everything you need is on the bed and I have selected some make-up for you which you'll see on the dresser. When you're ready you'll find me here in the lounge."

I found Mistress's bedroom and saw all the clothes I was expected to dress in, neatly laid on Mistress's bed. When dressed I did a less-than-perfect job of making up my face and putting on my wig. When I was satisfied with my appearance, well, I wasn't really satisfied with my appearance, but I did the best I could do and it was my first ever effort, I went gingerly downstairs to find Mistress Raven. Mistress Raven stood and smiled nicely at me as I entered the room. So did everybody else that was present.

"You must knock when entering a room and give me a curtsey, but never mind, come and sit down for a moment," Mistress Raven said patting the vacant seat on the sofa next to her.

"Today will be an assessment day where we can see if you're going to fit in with the household. We like to think we are an efficient and happy household, there will be discipline, but we are no ogres and we like to keep our servant staff and almost see them as family."

"How many slaves and maids have you?" I asked.

"If you join us there will be two full-time housemaids, you and Rebecca, whom I think you met last week, she is a TG like you.

"Yes, I did meet her," I replied.

"I know it doesn't sound much for a house this size, but we also have part-time servants and we put paid service slaves to good use as well. Apart from the housemaid, we have one lady's maid. She is a maid for Mistress Azure," Mistress said, pausing to catch her breath. "You won't see much of the lady's maid as she rarely leaves Mistress Azure's private quarters."

"Oh," I replied under my breath.

"You soon learn that it is common for lady's maids to rarely leave their Mistress's quarters. They are often restrained or locked in a bathroom when Mistress is out, then she can count on them always being there on call when she returns from a day out. This is something for you to bear in mind if you ever want a promotion to a lady's maid. Any questions Daisy about anything at all?" Mistress Raven asked.

"No, I don't think so, Mistress Raven," I replied

"Stand," she said. "I want to see how well you can curtsey." I stood and faced Mistress and attempted a curtsey. "You have not curtseyed before, have you, Daisy? Now let's try again, put your left foot behind your right. Go on do as

I say, putting one foot behind the other isn't hard." Mistress said, raising her voice slightly. I did as I was told, slightly shaken by her apparent change in attitude. "Now hold the sides of your skirt lightly and bob down and up as smoothly as you can." I curtsied several times and it took me a while to get the hang of it.

When Mistress was satisfied with my curtseying skills, she told me I must curtsey when entering and leaving a room and when spoken to. I was told not to worry too much today, but later if I take the position, forgetting to curtsey will be punishable as it will be considered slovenly and a lack of respect.

"I think you have enough skills to get you started so let's find you some work to do. You'll be surprised how time has flown already it is getting close to lunchtime and I had felt as if I had been here just ten minutes. So I think I will take you to the kitchen where you can start to make sandwiches for us all. Come with me, Daisy."

I followed Mistress to the kitchen which was missed out on my last tour of the house. I was surprised at how big it was, it looked more like a hotel kitchen than one would find in a home, but I suppose it was a very big house. Making sandwiches was a bigger task than I imagined. I wasn't just making a hand full of sandwiches I made plates and plates of them. Every now and again Rebecca would appear and take a couple of plates of sandwiches away to serve to the guests. When I had finished making sandwiches Mistress Raven came and found me.

"It's time to see what your cleaning skills are like," she said. "Follow me." I followed Mistress upstairs and I was left to clean a bathroom complete with a Jacuzzi. Mistress must have gone ahead of me as all the cleaning materials were there waiting for me to make use of.

“I think you can have this bathroom sparkling in about half an hour,” Mistress said glancing at her watch. “I’ll be back in thirty minutes to see how you’re getting on and check your work.” With those words, Mistress Raven disappeared leaving me to do my chores. I was still scrubbing when Mistress reappeared. I didn’t hear her arrive and I jumped out of my skin when she said out of the silence.

“Have you finished yet?” She laughed when she saw me jump. “You are a nervous little thing, aren’t you? I see you haven’t finished, but let’s see how well you have done so far.” Mistress Raven walked around the bathroom humming to herself as she inspected this and that.

"Well, it isn't good, is it? If you were full time this would have gotten you a trip to the basement for punishment, but today I will just point out your errors and then if you decide to join us you'll know the standards we expect from our slaves. First," she added, pointing to the mirrors, you need to get right into the corners. There is also scale around all the taps and the Jacuzzi nozzles that needs to go. Lastly, you don't just clean the top of the sink, you clean under it as well, the same with the toilet bowl and pedestal. I'll be back in another fifteen minutes and I expect all these errors to be sorted." With that Mistress disappeared again, leaving me with my tail between my legs as I reeled from the criticism.

When she reappeared she gave everything a cursory look and said:

“That’s better Daisy, right follow me. I followed her into what I knew to be her bedroom. I was surprised as it was still early afternoon and a bit soon to let me change and go home. However, I quickly realised this was not what I was here for.

“Last week I made a fuss of you Daisy, today it is payback time you will make a fuss of me. Pick up the hairbrush and brush my hair gently,” she warned with a slight rise in her voice. Note the word gently.

Mistress Raven was an attractive lady in her forties with an air of elegance about her. She looked after herself and was still quite trim and slender for her age with piercing dark blue eyes. She had shoulder-length black hair, hence her name Raven, I presumed. At close quarters I could smell her perfume as I brushed. I brushed and brushed and Mistress was almost in a purr of delight.

"Do you know what other duties a lady's maid has?" Mistress asked as I brushed.

"Um, help you with your makeup," I replied nervously.

"Anymore? Come on, there are lots of duties, use your imagination," Mistress urged.

"Manicure your nails," I replied.

"Yes, now you're getting into the spirit of things, come more ideas?" Mistress demanded.

"Cut your toenails, help you in the bath, help you dress and massage your feet when you return from shopping."

"That's a good girl, yes, all these things you have mentioned, but there is one more you have neglected to say," Mistress advised me.

"What is that Mistress?" I asked.

"Sexual services, you haven't mentioned sexual services," Mistress said as she turned her head to look at me as I brushed to see my facial response.

"Sexual services?" I repeated.

"Yes, a lady's maid will be expected to shave Mistress's pussy and after shaving go down between Mistress's legs and not come up until Mistress has had an orgasm or two."

"Oh," I replied, not having thought of such a thing.

"I tell you this Daisy because if you join us and do well as a maid of all work, I might at a later stage take you as my lady's maid. However, I am getting a bit ahead of myself you haven't agreed to join us yet." Mistress paused and was silent for a few moments and then said. "You are doing very well today, there is no need for a reply now, you may telephone in a day or two, but I am offering you the post of a maid."

"Thank you, Mistress, I replied. "I can tell you now?"

"No," Mistress Raven said, interrupting me, you think about it for a couple of days and let me know by telephone, we need to be both sure this is what you want. The position won't be filled until I hear from you. Now I am going to leave you here in the bedroom to change and go home."

Chapter Three

I went home a happy bunny, but it didn't take long for the reality to set in, what was I letting myself in for? All I did on the initiation day was make sandwiches, clean the bathroom badly and brush Mistress's hair. I was sure I would be expected to do much more once I was full-time. One half of my brain said all I will become is, an effeminate skivvy, the other half, the more forceful half of my brain said let's go for it as it is what I have been dreaming about for years. I had a deep psychotically need to be a slave and a preference to be a Victorian maid above all other aspects of B.D.S.M., I finally conclude these thoughts no matter how bizarre, filled almost my whole day, therefore it did make some sort of sense to act on them.

It was nevertheless three whole days before I took the plunge and rang Mistress Raven.

"I am so pleased to hear from you, Daisy. So why do I have the pleasure of your voice today?" She asked, fully anticipating my reply.

"I would like to take your offer of becoming a full-time maid," I replied sheepishly

"Good, good," Mistress replied down the phone, "I accept your offer, when can you start?

"I need to give notice on my bedsit," I replied and sort some other things out, so can I come a month from today?

"That's acceptable, Mistress said, "Then I expect to see you at 8 am on the 16th of next month. I have someone at the door, so you may go now I look forward to seeing you in a month." With that last remark, she rang off and I went home from the telephone kiosk feeling pleased I got the position and immediately began wondering what it would be like.

The month quickly passed and I gave notice at my lodgings. On my first day as a full-time maid, I arrived on time as usual, but it was different this time as I wasn't going home again at the end of the day, which took some coming to terms with. I felt extremely nervous and had last-minute cold feet and doubts about if I was doing the right thing. I could have changed my mind and left to go home, but no, that would be silly, I am here now and with trepidation, I went up to the door and rang the bell, I was now committed, no going back. Mistress Raven as usual answered the door herself.

“Daisy come on in and you’re spot on time again I am impressed. Right, let’s get you changed straight away so up you go to the bedroom and I will be up shortly.” I thanked Mistress and immediately made my way to the bedroom and began to change as all my clothes were laid out on the bed ready for me. I noticed this time I had proper silicone falsies so no need to use my socks. It felt strangely odd when dressed it occurred to me this is how I will be dressed from now on. In about half an hour Mistress Raven appeared. She looked at me approvingly.

"Right fold up and give me all your old clothes they will be given to the charity shop in the town, you won't need male clothes anymore. I did so and Mistress disappeared briefly and returned minus the clothes.

"Daisy now you dressed, made-up and ready for the day, follow me, I'll show you to the maid's quarters," Mistress said. I followed her up into the attic some five floors up. Mistress showed me into a tiny room barely big enough for a single bed.

"I know it is small," Mistress said, but you won't be spending much time in here I promise you." Mistress put down some additional clothes on the bed. "I have some clothes for you as I imagine you only have the uniform provided, and you'll need a change of clothes when these go in the wash. In amongst the clothes I've put on the bed you'll find spare panties and a couple of nighties, if there is anything I have missed let me know?"

"Laundry will be one of your duties, by the way." She added with a smile.

I noticed when we left my room there was a ceramic plaque on my door with the words "Maids Room". As we walked away I saw another room with the same plaque which I assumed was Rebecca's room. We went back downstairs to the living room. I was told to sit on the sofa.

"Rebecca," Mistress shouted. Almost in a flash, Rebecca the maid arrived. "A pot of tea for two," she said. Rebecca without a word curtseyed and left the room.

"I expect you are very thirsty after your journey, so we shall both enjoy a cup of tea and while we are drinking I will explain a few rules so everything runs smoothly and there won't be any problems or misunderstandings. Problems that persist are usually sorted downstairs in the basement."

It didn't seem two minutes before Rebecca returned with a pot of tea on a tray and placed it on the table in front of us.

"Will that be all Mistress?" she asked.

"Yes, that's fine, thank you, Rebecca." Rebecca nodded and gave a respectful curtsey and left the room.

"Yes, where were we, Daisy?" Mistress asked as she recollected her thoughts. "Oh yes rules, lots of rules. You now know how to curtsey, do you remember when you are expected to curtsey?

"Yes, I think so, Mistress," I replied.

"Good," Mistress Raven said, "and you realise you curtsey not only to me, but all the Masters and Mistresses if they address you, or you enter a room where a Master or Mistress is present.

"Yes," Mistress I replied in agreement.

"I know having to curtsey is a bit of a chore, but you'll quickly get used to it and think nothing of it after a while. The next rule is you're allowed to sit in the kitchen at any time, but you're not allowed to sit on any of the furniture elsewhere in the house unless you have express permission. You may be requested to sit or kneel on the floor at times. Do you understand?"

"Yes Mistress," I replied.

The next rule is you only ever speak when someone addresses you. You never speak out of turn. You also always keep your eyes cast down. You would have noticed that Rebecca never looks directly at me, as to do so is taken as being disrespectful. Lots of rules I know we won't be too strict on you for your first week so you may get used to our ways. The next regulation is you always start the day with clean, fresh and ironed clothes. This includes wiping and polishing your shoes. You'll always be nicely made up and have clean, manicured hands and nails. The last rule that I can think of at this minute is no chatting with the other staff unless it is a tea break. Tips you must never seem to be doing nothing, always look busy or come and ask for more chores."

Mistress asked me if I had any questions. While we drank tea Mistress asked me about my journey and if I had put all my affairs in order and I was told I won't be allowed to leave the house, except in very exceptional circumstances. I was also told there was a small courtyard I could use during my breaks if I want some fresh air.

"It is time to get you started. I was told to vacuum all five hallways and dust the skirting boards and dust the top of pictures, starting at the top of the house in the attic and working my way downstairs. Whilst I was busy vacuuming Rebecca darted over and in a hushed voice said:

"Have you started full-time today?" Yes, I replied.

"Be careful Mistress Raven may seem all sweetness and light now, but she will slowly change and she doesn't spare the cane, so you have been warned. Chat more later," she said, looking around herself furtively before disappearing again, leaving me to continue with my duties.

Chapter Four

Perhaps not too surprising my days were filled with drudgery. It was a long succession of vacuum cleaning, changing beds, and cleaning bathrooms, bedrooms and kitchen. On top of all this, I was in sole charge of the laundry. I didn't mind laundry so much as no one came into the utility room and I could skive a little and take rests as I watched the washing spinning around in the machines. I also found ironing took less energy than some of my tasks and I used to stretch it out.

I hadn't experienced much in the way of punishment, just the odd terse word from Mistress Raven. However, I was quick to notice as the days went by Mistress was getting much stricter with me, much more so than she was with Rebecca. I suppose I got the extra unwanted attention because I was new.

My first trip to the basement was on my fifth day at the house. I had just finished vacuuming four floors I was absolutely exhausted and sat on the carpet beside my vacuum cleaner only for a moment. Out of the blue yonder, a Mistress I didn't know personally came into the corridor. She was a new Mistress who had just joined the household. I didn't hear her come and was rising to my feet when she announced:

"What is your name maid?" she asked in a condescending voice, looking at me as if I was something nasty trodden into the carpet.

"Daisy," I said as I started the vacuum cleaner up again.

"Well Daisy," she replied. I shall be reporting you to Mistress Raven for neglecting your duties. The Mistress, whom I later found out, was Mistress Dorado, walked past me and that was the last I saw of her that day. But when I finished my duties and reported to Mistress Raven, I soon found out Mistress Dorado hadn't forgotten my misdemeanour and did report me.

"Here Daisy," barked Mistress Raven, " kneel here before my feet and explain why Mistress Dorado found you sitting on the hall carpet looking as if you might have been sleeping?"

"I just sat down for a moment," I replied.

"Was it your break period?" Mistress asked fully well knowing the answer. For if it was my break period I would have come downstairs to the kitchen for a cup of tea.

"No," Mistress I replied.

At that point in the conversation, Rebecca appears and told Mistress she was wanted on the telephone.

"I can't deal with you this minute Daisy, go down to the basement and find yourself a wall to stand against with your hands on your head until I return," said Mistress as she went off with the maid.

I went down into the basement, which was empty of people. I looked around with trepidation at the array of B.D.S.M., equipment which was everywhere. I found a vacant wall and stood against it with my hands on my head. Within minutes I heard Mistress come down the basement wooden steps. She didn't speak initially. Instead, I heard her fumble with things on a table.

"Right Daisy, you can turn around now. You know what you're here for to be punished. Step forward," she demanded. I stepped up to the table.

"If you look you'll see I have three implements on the table, a riding crop, a cane and a strap. I am going to be kind to you as this is your first punishment, I shall let you choose which I shall use today." I looked at the implements and didn't favour any of them, they all looked to be capable of giving me intense pain. "I can't wait all day, I have other things to do than just chastise you, Daisy. Choose now?" Not knowing what to choose I picked up the strap and passed it to Mistress.

"Good choice," Mistress said, folding the leather strap into two. Come over here to the spanking bench. Um, I think maybe you should be restrained for your first strapping. I don't want you wriggling and putting your hands in the way." She put down the strap and put cuffs on my wrists and ankles, then she got me to bend over the bench and attached my arms and legs to the frame.

"That's better she said. What you'll soon realise is I do enjoy punishing my maids, I do get quite a thrill in watching you suffer. However, this is your first punishment ever, so I won't be too hard on you, you'll get six of the strap. Mistress pulled up my skirt. "All punishment," Mistress Raven added, " is on the bare flesh. Then she pulled down my tights and panties. I felt the leather of the strap lightly touch my bottom as Mistress aimed.

Just as the punishment was about to begin Maid Rebecca came down the basement steps and said.

"Sorry to disturb you, Mistress," but the man you spoke to is back on the phone."

"Okay Rebecca, I'll be right up," she replied then she addressed me. "You'll have to wait until I have taken my call. I will leave the strap where you can see it, so you can think about the delights that await you." With that Mistress left the strap on the bench in front of me and left with Rebecca. The strap looked like a mean piece of equipment and was solid cow leather and about eighteen inches wide and approximately just under a quarter of an inch thick. It was impossible to imagine this strap being used on my bottom. I was beginning to wish for Mistress Raven's return to get my punishment over with.

Mistress wasn't gone very long, but it was agony looking at this thick strap, as there was no doubt it was going to hurt a great deal. My Mistress came down the steps and walked over to me and picked up the strap.

"I bet you want to get this over with don't you Daisy? So it is six of the best. I warn you, in the future, it will be many more strokes. I am only giving you six because you're new to all this." Then before I could absorb what she said down came the strap. The pain was more than I ever imagined and I let out a very loud scream.

"Don't be such a baby you have five more to come yet.

"Do I have to have another five strokes?" I begged.

"Yes, you do that is the whole nature of punishment to give you something you don't like, it will teach you not to sit down on the job. With that comment, I got the next five strokes. I was wriggling mass of pain when the punishment finished.

"That hurt didn't it?" Mistress Raven said, kissing me on the cheek. I bet you won't be so keen to come down to the basement in the future. It's all done now, we can be friends again, the punishment is over." With that, I was released from the spanking bench and sent back to my chores.

The next punishment was a different sort. A couple of weeks later I was chatting with Rebecca in the kitchen as we both made sandwiches for lunchtime. While we nattered away Mistress Raven came to the door while we were facing the other way. When we turned we saw her arm resting against the door frame as she watched us with a look on her face which said all.

"Shouldn't you two be working she asked?" We both immediately apologised, curtseyed and promised to get on with the sandwich-making. "Just wait there, I'll be back in a few minutes," Mistress said, turning to go back from whence she came. Around five minutes later she returned and without a word she came up behind me and popped a ball gag in my mouth, then she went over to Rebecca and did the same. Then, without a word being said she left.

We continued with our work with the humiliating ball gags on and was quite a spectacle for all the Masters and Mistress to see and snigger at our discomfort. We also missed lunch and dinner because we could eat and it wasn't until 8 pm when Mistress Raven took the ball gags out, leaving me with a very sore mouth for the remainder of the day. Mistress Raven seemed to have satisfied her need to punish and humiliate us.

One morning she called both me and Rebecca into the living room. We both stood to attention in front of her and gave a respectful curtsey and waited to hear why we had been summoned.

"I have two things to say. First, I am very happy with you and you both have been promoted from full-time maids to lifetime maids. In other words, if we have to sell up and downsize, we will keep you two on regardless. After all, I am not about to start doing my own housework.

“Thank you, Madam,” Rebecca replied. I didn’t say anything but smiled to show my approval.

“The other thing is it has started to bug me that you both wear different uniforms. They are completely different, but Rebecca’s is above the knee while your’s Daisy is way slightly below the knee. They are also different styles as well. To my mind, that isn’t uniform. To be a proper uniform your dresses need to be exactly the same. So what I have done as you're now both lifelong maids is to get you both a matching uniform at the house’s expense.”

Mistress held up one to show us. It was an Edwardian maid’s uniform, plain and midi in length, very different from what we had been wearing.

"I felt the uniforms we were wearing was a bit too fetish, especially as we both are the real thing and not here playing at being a maid to satisfy a fantasy like some of our guests." Mistress Raven said, passing the new dresses to me and Rebecca To go with the uniform was a frilly petticoat, an apron and a frilly cap to wear on our heads. We were told to take the uniforms, two each, and go away and change and report back to Mistress Raven for her approval.

I was delighted in a way I didn't like our uniforms to my mind they did seem to acknowledge to the world we were engaged in real housework, work and not running around with a feather duster pretending to be maids for a fee.

When dressed I looked in the full-length mirror and I looked very much the part and I gave myself a little curtsey for effect. I met Rebecca in the hall and we admired how we both looked before going off downstairs to find Mistress Raven.

Downstairs we found Mistress Raven in the living room reading a magazine with her feet up on the sofa looking very relaxed. We stood before her and curtsied in unison. Mistress looked over her magazine, sat up and beamed a smile.

"Oh yes, oh yes, you both look gorgeous, much better than I ever imagined," Mistress said. She shouted to Brian, the man of the house, and he emerged in his dressing gown. I don't think I have ever seen him out of a smoking jacket or dressing gown. Brian came over and looked us both up and down.

"Money well spent," he said in a gruff voice and disappeared back from where he came from. He was not a man of many words. Before Rebecca and I were sent off to our duties Mistress Raven took several photos of us both.

Chapter Five

Life returned to a normal life of monotonous drudgery. I had one day forgotten to dust one of the skirting boards and was hauled up to the housekeeper Mistress Raven. She admonished me and said I was to be punished. Mistress Raven at the time was entertaining another lady who was new to the B.D.S.M., scene and was learning the ropes as a dominant. I guessed she was much older than me, mid-thirties and was very, very attractive. She had a nice nimble frame and great legs, she had a quite sweet, pure face and it was difficult to see her being dominant to a slave.

“Mistress Tina, would you like to punish my maid for me?” Mistress asked looking at her guest.

“Oh, I don’t know,” Mistress Tina said, “I don’t want to interfere with your domestic arrangements.

“Oh, nonsense It will be a good experience for you,” Mistress Raven assured her guest.

“I suppose it is a good opportunity, perhaps one I should take advantage of. What punishment should I give your maid?” Mistress Tina asked.

“That’s entirely up to you Mistress Tina you heard Daisy is guilty of missing a skirting board while she was cleaning. I’ll let you judge what punishment is appropriate for such an offence. Go on, off you go, take Daisy down to the basement, all the equipment is there, when she has been punished bring her back to me. Go on, go and enjoy yourself.”

Mistress Tina thanked her host and stood beckoning me to follow her. I was quite nervous, as far as I was concerned, it is better a devil you know than someone you don't. Mistress Tiny may enjoy herself, but I was fairly sure I wasn't going to. Although Mistress Tina was a little slip of a thing, it doesn't mean she can't be cruel. I followed the lady downstairs to the basement and stood waiting while she looked at all the equipment that was available to her.

"It's a bit of an Aladdin's cave," Mistress Tina said to herself, "I am spoilt for choice." The Mistress walked around the basement taking in all the B.D.S.M., delights and settled on the St Andrews cross. "Strip off," she ordered, everything down to your birthday suit."

I slowly took my clothes off to the annoyance of Mistress Tina, who was itching to get started on me. Once undressed, I was told to go and put my back on the cross. When I did so she fastened me spread eagle to the cross.

"Um, what shall we do with you first," she said. "I know." With that comment went off to a table and brought back two nipple clamps connected by a heavy stainless steel chain. Mistress Tina massaged my nipple and twisted and turned them until they began to feel sore and erect, then she placed the clamps on each nipple, which made me wince which pleased Mistress especially when she let the chain hang loose. Then for added effect, she picked up the chain again and pulled it which had me screaming for her to stop.

"Oh, I see you like that," she said, giving me another tug. "Look," she said your penis is getting harder, it doesn't like being left out it wants to join in the fun. Let's see what we can do about it." Mistress casually walked back to the table and picked up a riding crop. "This will do nicely," she said, bending it almost in two as she walked back to me. She began to whip my penis with the leather flap on the end of the crop. In between times, she tugged on the nipple clamp chain for effect. The pain was beyond description.

"Your penis is getting harder it likes the crop. Well, you can have too much of a good thing, let's try something else." She released me from the cross and removed the nipple clamps which hurt more than putting them on. My nipples throbbed intensely for ages after the clamps had been removed. Mistress massaged my nipples before taking me over to a medieval wooden stock that secured the head, wrists and feet. Mistress Tina got me to step into the stock and fastened my feet, then I had to rest my head and wrists on the cutouts and she lowered the top ıalf of the stock until I was completely ·estrained.

'Well finished you off with the cane I think, :hen you can go back to work." Mistress Tina vent off to select a cane and returned to me. Without any ceremony, she gave me twelve strokes in very quick succession which had me vriggling and screaming once more begging her :o stop.

'That's it," Mistress said, "you're sorted. I'll let you out of this contraption and we can go back ıpstairs." Mistress went up the steps first and I followed, the basement steps came right up into :he living room. Mistress Raven smiled at Mistress Tina and said:

'It sounded up here as if you were having fun," she remarked to Mistress Tiny.

"Yes," she replied. Thank you I quite enjoyed myself and your maid is now suitably punished.

"Good," Mistress Raven agreed.

"One thing I think you should know," Mistress Tina said. Daisy's penis got hard during the punishment. I strongly suspect she plays with herself habitually. I am sure you don't want her wasting valuable energy on self-satisfaction when her energy is needed for domestic work, so you may want to look into this?" Mistress Tina concluded.

"Yes, thank you for alerting me to this," Mistress Raven said, "yes indeed I will be giving this some thought." I was then released to get on with my chores and go and clean offending the skirting boards again. I didn't think any more about Mistress Tina's remarks about my penis until one day a week or two later I was summoned to the living room where Mistress Raven was waiting.

“Oh, here you are Daisy, I have been waiting for you,” Mistress Raven said beckoning me closer. I gave Mistress a nice smooth curtsey to impress and stepped closer. “I have something for you,” Mistress said with a mischievous smile. First, though take this saucer and go and sit on the armchair in the corner and masturbate for me. Take your time and have a good orgasm as it will be your very last. When you cum, cum on the saucer and bring it to me, don’t waste any.” Mistress pointed to the armchair and off I went. Masturbating in a busy living room with lots of strangers coming and going wasn’t easy. I had a job to maintain a hard-on, in fact, most of the time my penis was as soft as jelly. My penis was suffering from stage fright, but eventually, I managed to blot everyone out and after a good hour came on the saucer. It was a bumper orgasm and I took the semen over to Mistress Raven.

“ At long last, Good girl,” Mistress Raven said. “That’s a lot of semen a good two, three teaspoons worth, I would say. Now lick the saucer dry she said. No point in wasting good semen, especially as it is your last. I felt humiliated licking the seamen of the saucer in front of so many people.

“Right,” Mistress Raven said. “Come here and stand in front of me drop your tights and knickers and stand with your feet as wide apart as you can. As I did so Mistress unpacked a box and produced a chrome metal cage and began to attach it to my penis and balls. Mistress fiddled away with my private parts, which produced a mixture of sensations, warm hands and a cold metal cage.

“I chose this chastity device because it is easy to clean when on,” Mistress said as she fiddled with the device, “That is important as you’ll never take it off and not be able to masturbate again, so I do hope you enjoyed your orgasm as that was your last, ever. Maids should be totally selfless and you shouldn't be allowed to pleasure themselves and waste valuable energy. You're here for one purpose only and that is to make our lives easier and more comfortable not your own. Your comforts have no concern to us at all. If you get any joy from serving us it is entirely coincidental. Now go back to your work."

I went back to my chores. It felt really funny and uncomfortable to walk with this contraption attached to me, it felt cumbersome. But like all things I did eventually get used to it with time. It was a slow and stealthy punishment in itself. As the days wore on I felt the need to masturbate more and more. I was on heat all the time. I tried all sorts of ways to remove the device without success. Indeed, it was a bad idea to arouse myself as the penis would grow, but have nowhere to go and that was very painful. Mistress Raven would have known all this and would no doubt get a thrill about my permanent discomfort and agony.

Life returned to a 12-hour day of drudgery just a succession of cleaning, polishing, sweeping and making sandwiches for lunch. I hadn’t actually seen that much of Mistress Raven except to get my daily instructions. Then one day whilst making sandwiches I was summoned from the kitchen and asked to report to Mistress Raven in the living room as soon as I could.

Chapter Six

I made my way to the living room and knocked to enter. I stepped up to Mistress Raven and gave her a respectful curtsey.

"Oh, here you are come and sit down next to me on the sofa," she insisted patting the seat next to her. "I have something to say to you," she added smiling. It was the sort of smile that had me on edge as I knew something was afoot and it may not be something I would like.

"I expect Daisy you have heard the gossip in the servant's quarters about the house having some financial difficulties?"

"Yes Mistress Raven," I replied there has been gossip, but I didn't necessarily believe it."

"Well, it is true to a point, but don't worry your position is secure no matter what. But that is not to say you can't do your bit to help relieve the financial burden," Mistress said stopping to pause and see my reaction.

"How can I do that?" I asked, "I don't earn anything. I have no money not so much as a penny." I replied somewhat bemused.

"Well, do you recall a gentleman who comes and spends time with us on Tuesdays usually? You might remember him because he is a bit stout and always wears bright clothes and a dicky bow tie. He is quite distinctive"

"Oh yes, I think I know the chap you mean," I replied. "He likes to talk a lot."

" Yes, you have the right person. Well, his name is Michael, he has taken a shine to you," Mistress Raven said.

"A shine to me?" I replied, feeling very much on edge.

"Yes, you should feel faltered and he is willing to pay for you and if you do well, he might see you regularly, which will help the house's finances." Mistress Raven went on to say, sensing I wouldn't be best pleased with this revelation and want to resist it.

"This isn't in my contract with you Mistress," I said not knowing what else to say other than I wanted to wriggle out of the dilemma

"Now that's not strictly true," Mistress Raven conceded. "However, you did agree to be totally obedient. If I told you to go down on one of my visiting gentlemen, you would do as you're told, wouldn't you?"

"Yes Mistress," I replied reluctantly. Then what is the difference, except Michael is paying me for the privilege of your company? As a reward, you will get a day off drudgery and can spend Tuesday here in the living room reading magazines and drinking coffee until your guest arrives. So it isn't all bad is it, now go and get on with your duties."

I left Mistress and went back to the kitchen feeling very unhappy about the new development. When Tuesday arrived, I was taken off my duties and told to report to the living room. When I arrived Mistress Raven told me to relax and pour a coffee and select a magazine or two while I wait for my guest to arrive. Secretly, I hoped my "guest" wouldn't show. Although I admit it was nice to have a day of just lounging around reading and chatting as the Masters and Mistresses do. At least it was an opportunity to recharge my batteries as a twelve-hour day, with no days off, scrubbing and cleaning takes its toll.

I almost felt sorry for Rebecca, who had the work of two today, as she was sure to have to do my chores as well as her own. My guest Michael was supposed to arrive at 1 pm but is late, so I began to relax thinking he may have changed his mind and was not coming. It was wishful thinking though, as ten minutes later he came into the living room puffing and panting. He apologised profusely saying he got stuck in traffic. The man's apology was readily accepted and he was given a cup of coffee and offered a seat opposite me.

After a bit of general chit-chat, Mistress Raven said to me:

"Daisy why don't you show Michael to the "guest" bedroom as I am sure he would like to get to know you better." Mistress could sense my reluctance and urged me to stand and take Michael away. I stood and so too did Michael.

"Take your time Michael enjoy yourself, there is no rush, you're not on the clock today, this is an introductory offer," Mistress said, urging me to take Michael's hand and lead him off to the bedroom. There was no going back now so I just had to grin and bare what was going to happen to me.

“I’ve been wanting you for weeks,” Michael said when we reached the bedroom.” I didn’t think you were available until one day whilst I was chatting to Mistress Raven and she said yes, I could have you for a price so I agreed. Whilst he was talking, he dropped his pants and out came an already erect penis. “I’ve been waiting for this for so long, come on Daisy get sucking, let’s see how good you are?” I held his penis in one hand and began to suck. Fortunately, the man was so pent up and aroused, that he didn’t take long to come directly into my mouth. Two or three salty gushes and it was all over and I could relax.

“Oh yes,” he said, “that was every bit as good as I hoped. “I shall book you every Tuesday, next time we have a go at anal sex, and see how that goes." Michael spent the next half an hour fondling me on the bed and then we dressed and returned to the living room.

'Oh, here you are," said Mistress Raven. "I hope daisy didn't disappoint?" she asked Michael.

'No, I would like to book her every Tuesday if I may," Michael said.

'Yes of course that's excellent, we'll make a standing note in the diary for you. Don't forget to tell your friends about Daisy, the more the merrier.

'Yes, I shall," Michael said discreetly passing a wad of notes to Mistress Raven before leaving. Mistress Raven showed him out. When Micheal had gone Mistress returned to the living room and said to me:

“You have been a very good girl, go and pour yourself a coffee and tell me all about it. Micheal told me at the front door, that he is going to recommend you to some of his friends. This revelation needless to say didn’t have me jumping with joy. Soon I was getting bookings, for two, or three days a week as I became more popular with the “guests”. Poor Rebecca couldn’t cope with all the extra work, so Mistress Raven began looking for an additional maid to join the household.

Chapter Seven

Finding an additional maid to join us was easier said than done and most applicants were not genuine and were just people looking for a cheap thrill. Finally, Mistress Raven recruited a TG maid called Mimi. However, it wasn’t long after that disaster struck the house which changed everything.

The house had received a letter from the council stating they have had numerous complaints from the neighbours about frequent male visitors. The letter went on to say the house will be monitored and unless the complaints cease they will send someone to investigate. This letter needless to say set the cat amongst the pigeons and everyone was in a state of panic. All premium services stopped dead that day. This was a major relief for me but I did worry about the future ahead as the house budget was now going to be massively reduced. Although I did console myself with having been told Rebecca and I will be kept on regardless of future circumstances.

I didn't ask Mistress Raven about my future because quite frankly, I was frightened too.

Also, maids were so lowly nothing was discussed directly with us. Rebecca and I had to glean what was happening by overhearing conversations and gossip. The weeks went on and as I was no longer needed for personal duties I was back to long laborious hours as a domestic maid. My work was, however, slightly lighter since Mimi had been taken on, now maid duties were shared between the three of us. I did wonder about how long Mimi would be kept if finances got tight, after all, she was one extra mouth to feed.

My concerns came to a head when one day I was called into the living room to see Mistress Raven. I was worried it was to be punished as earlier that day I accidentally kicked over a bucket of soapy water and flooded a corridor, although it was sorted quite quickly and no damage was done. Nevertheless, with so many people in the house, the transgression was soon brought to Mistress's attention and I thought I was summoned to Mistress Raven to be punished.

To my delight Mistress, Raven smiled at me as I came into the living room. I assumed she would hardly smile at me if she was about to scold and beat me.

"Come and sit down," she said. "We need to talk about the future and the house's reduced budget," Mistress Raven said, but qualified it by adding," you do not need to worry, we are not dispensing with your services, you're a lifetime slave that has been established, but there is a need to change."

"Oh, I see," I said when I hadn't seen at all, "what are these changes?"

"That's what I want to discuss with you. You'll remember in better times we took on extra help in the form of maid Mimi."

"Yes, I remember," I agreed, "does that mean she now has to leave?"

"Maybe, but not necessarily," Mistress Raven replied with a sigh. The reduced house budget will only go as far as keeping two full-time maids."

"I don't understand," I replied, "surely that means one of us has to leave, but Rebbeca has been assured she too is a lifetime maid?" I said reminding Mistress of her commitment.

"Yes, yes, yes, keep your hair on Daisy, as I already said your positions are safe and there is a way out of this predicament," Mistress went on to say, "and that concerns you?" Mistress stopped and suggested we had a cup of tea before explaining more and shouted for Rebecca who quickly attended.

"A pot of tea for two Rebbeca, please," ordered Mistress. "We'll continue the conversation vhen the tea arrives. A few moments later and Rebecca returned carrying a tray, she gave a quick, respectful bob and placed the tray between us. Then she asked if Mistress Raven needed anything else, and on a negative Rebecca bobbed again and left the room closing the living room door behind her.

"I waited," Mistress Raven explained, "because I don't want the world to know what I am going to say next." Mistress stopped talking again to pour the tea for us both.

"How do you feel about becoming my lady's maid?" she asked. That took me by complete surprise and it was not a request I was expecting.

"I don't know what to say, Mistress, I replied, "this has taken me by surprise.

"The thing is if you become my lady's maid, I finance you, you are my maid and my responsibility, not the house's. Then we can keep maid Mimi on as there will still be only two housemaids on the household expenses, Mimi and Rebecca. You'll be my maid and no longer have anything to do with the house. What do you think? It is a lot to take in, I know."

"I'm not sure," I replied, feeling a bit overwhelmed. "I've not had time to give the prospect some thought, it is all a bit sudden."

"Do you remember the conversation we had a few weeks ago, where we talked about a lady's maid's duties?" Mistress asked.

"Yes, I remember," I replied.

"Can you recall what they are?" Mistress asked. I was a bit slow in replying, so Mistress helped me out.

"Your function is to attend to all your Mistress's needs, no matter what they may be. For example, you're to serve me breakfast in bed. Dress me, brush my hair, help me bathe, scrub my back etcetera. You will also at times serve me my lunch and dinner in my room. Of course, you will also have to keep my bedroom and ensuite bathroom absolutely spotless."

"I heard lady's maids have to stay in their Mistress's bedroom at all times, is that so?" I asked.

"Yes, you're to be at my beck and call constantly, you'll only leave the room to go to the kitchen to fetch food for your Mistress. At all other times, you're to remain locked in my room when I go down to the living room or go out for the day. You'll be my slave your entire life will be devoted to me. So what do you say?"

"I still don't know," I replied, "I need time to think about it," I replied a little agitated by the need to decide so quickly. It was a kind of insidious bullying that Mistress seized on deliberately.

"Daisy you take your time deciding, but we need to decide about Mimi's future. The house will have to let her go today unless you agree to become my lady's maid." Mistress said, turning the emotional screws. "It will be a great shame to let Mimi go as she is settling down so well." Mistress mused. "You like Mimi don't you?" Mistress asked.

"Yes," I replied.

"Then you won't want to see her turned on the streets today, made homeless and without any money, will you? If you don't decide very soon I shall have to send for her and tell her the bad news. I am sure she will be very upset and cry, but it is one of those things." Mistress assured me, mounting pressure for me to agree and become her lady's maid. "A lady's maid is considered a promotion Daisy, it is considered a station above a maid of all work."

"If I agree when do I start?"

"Immediately, I will send you straight up to my room and you can clean and tidy it for me to come up later for lunch," Mistress replied. "Does that mean you accept the position?"

There was one thing that was niggling me in the back of my mind. When I was a housemaid, I only saw Mistress Raven occasionally when she allotted Rebecca and me chores and for the administration of punishment. I knew her to be very domineering and very strict. If I was to become her lady's maid, I'll be in her company for much of the day there will be very little respite. However, I also didn't want to be the one responsible for maid Mimi to have to leave and felt I didn't really have a choice.

“Yes, I agree to be your lady’s maid,” I replied reluctantly.

“Good girl, now you go up to my room and give it a good clean from top to bottom. I’ll be up later and we can talk some more about your new duties.” Mistress said, pointing towards the door. I could see she was very pleased with her new acquisition and couldn’t wait to start training me. I left Mistress Raven and went up to her room. The room was quite big with a large double bed, two walk-in wardrobes and a dressing table. The was also a sofa, coffee table and a tiny kitchenette for making snacks and coffee. In addition to this, there was an ensuite bathroom with a Jacuzzi.

The rooms were luxurious but in an untidy state, Mistress was obviously very disorganised and now she has me will probably get worse knowing I am there to clear up. It was early fternoon and I set about tidying and cleaning he room, it was nearly five pm before Mistress rrived.

'Oh yes," she said, the bedroom looks a lot idier than when I left it. I won't inspect your vork today I give you a chance to settle into our new role. Mimi asked me to tell you she is ery grateful you have become my lady's maid, o she may continue as a maid. See, you have nade two people very happy, me and Mimi. Oh, ne thing Daisy," Mistress said in afterthought. 'In future when I come into the room you'll tand and give me a respectful curtsey. Don't orget."

Mistress sat down at the dressing table, made erself comfortable and passed me her hair rush.

'You may brush my hair as we chat," Mistress aid waiting for me to begin brushing. Mistress had slightly wiry hair that was prone to knots and brushing her hair free of knots was quite a feat.

"If you look behind you at the foot of my bed you'll see a brand new foam dog basket. It is quite comfortable I chose it myself this morning when I went shopping. That is where you'll sleep at night, so you're on hand if I need you. You may use the toilet at night without my permission. I have also emptied a section of my wardrobe so you may store your clothes. Here," she added opening a drawer of the dresser, is where you may keep your makeup. Everything is to be kept in this one drawer and not lying around to get mixed up with my makeup or I'll get very annoyed with you and you won't like that. Any question so far daisy?"

No Mistress," I replied as I brushed.

“Good. First thing in the morning while I am still sleeping, you’ll dress and makeup and go to the kitchen to get my breakfast, which is usually two lightly boiled eggs and two pieces of medium toast cut into strips. Whilst in the kitchen you may have a bowl of cereal. I don’t expect you to be out of the room for more than twenty minutes. Coffee will be made here in the room when you return. I take milk and one sugar. You may also make yourself a coffee. Understand so far?” Mistress asked in an authoritative tone of voice.

“Yes Mistress,” I replied.

“That’s good, you had better be paying attention,” Mistress warned. “We will be learning together as believe it or not you’re my first ever lady’s maid and I intend to make a total success out of you.”

When I leave in the morning to go downstairs, you'll be either locked in the bathroom or the bedroom if they are both to be cleaned whilst I am downstairs. I'll return usually at lunchtime. I will have pre-ordered my lunch and all you have to do is go to the kitchen and collect it. Your lunch will be whatever I leave on my plate. When you have eaten you'll take the dirty dishes down to the kitchen and return, no dilly-dallying." After lunch, I may require some personal service depending on how I feel. Dinner time is a repeat of lunchtime."

I was then sent off to my room to collect my things and when I returned I was allowed to put all my stuff away in my part of the wardrobe and the dresser drawer. I was told to keep out my nightie and change into it as it was getting late.

Chapter Eight

I didn't get much sleep the first night, needless to say, I wasn't used to sleeping in a dog basket at the foot of the bed. The dog basket would have been quite comfortable and plush had I been a dog, but I was too big for it and had to scrunch myself up into the foetal position. I was also afraid to cough, sneeze and toss and turn in case it upset Mistress. Whilst I lay there awake, I noticed mistress slept well as I could hear her quietly snooze the night away.

Morning came not too soon and I got up and quietly walked around the room and got my makeup bag and went to the bathroom. I held my hand under the tap to dampen the noise of water splashing. When I was made-up and dressed I tiptoed to the door and made my way down to the kitchen. When I returned with the breakfast tray I didn't know quite what to do with it, whether to place it on the bed, bedside table or where. Fortunate Mistress stirred.

"Ah, here you are," she sat up and beckoned me to put the breakfast tray on her lap. "I am remiss, I hadn't told you the morning protocol. In future when you return to the breakfast tray and I am still sleeping, you will put the tray down on the bedside table and shake my pillow until I wake, you're not, I repeat not, allowed to shout at me or touch me without express permission."

"Yes Mistress," I replied.

"Well, curtsey," Mistress admonished. I won't be letting you off for these indiscretions for long. In fact, I have decided I will punish you, it is better to nip these things in the bud straight away than let them fester. Go to the end of the bed." Mistress ordered. I did as I was told.

'Now put your arms out straight at your side ınd keep them there as high as you can, until I ell you otherwise. I will be gentle with you, to)egin with, whilst you learn my ways. You'll ılready let your arms slip after two seconds, put hem back up," she shouted. "You'll stay like hat until I have eaten my breakfast."

don't know about being gentle it was only noments before my arms began to tire and I onged to put them down at my side. Every now ınd again Mistress would look up from her)reakfast and beckon me to raise my arms with ı gesture from her hands. However, as time vent on my arms began to sink and no matter ıow hard I tried I couldn't raise them up)roperly. Just as I gave up and put my arms lown at my side out of necessity Mistress inished her breakfast, didn't seem to notice and old me to take the tray back down to the ‹itchen.

When I returned to Mistress's room, she said:

"Your punishment wasn't too bad, was it? Don't think for one moment I will always let you off so lightly," Mistress said smiling. "Go inside the wardrobe and you'll see an umbrella basket. If you look, in it you'll see a dragon cane bring it to me." I did as I was told and rummaged through the umbrella until I saw the cane and pulled it out. I took it to Mistress who was still sitting up in bed. Mistress took it from me and whisked it a couple of times so I could tremble at the whooshing sound.

"This is all I need for your chastisement, I don't need a whole basement of implements, I enjoy using a cane. Believe me, this is enough to ensure your perfect obedience. I don't need anything else. If I use this full strength, you'll know all about it and won't want a repeat for a very long time. Right put the cane away back in the wardrobe," Mistress said, "I don't suppose it will be long before your first introduction. At least you now know where it is if I ask you to fetch it. Don't worry, it won't always be the cane I have a whole arsenal of exquisite non-corporeal punishments for a lazy lady's maid."

My next duty was to help Mistress Raven dress. I helped with her bra, and stockings and button her dress at the back. Then I watched Mistress put on the minimum of makeup and then I brushed her hair.

"I'm off downstairs now to spend some time in the living room. It is quite tidy in here still but you can go and clean the bathroom. I stepped into the bathroom and heard the door lock behind me.

"You'll have to get used to being locked in from now on, at least there is the toilet if you need it, and I'll be back at lunchtime," Mistress said from the other side of the door as she left the bedroom.

I cleaned the bathroom and then there was nothing to do but sit on the edge of the Jacuzzi whilst I waited for Mistress's return. It occurred to me a lady's maid had to have the patience of a saint. I soon discovered, that doing nothing, was almost as bad as being worked to the bone. Boredom makes time pass very, very slowly. Eventually, I heard Mistress return and she immediately unlocked the bathroom door.

"Right Daisy," she said go and fetch my lunch from the kitchen. Whilst you're gone, I will inspect your work."

I immediately left for the kitchen. In the kitchen, I found Mistress's lunch on the hot plate as there were no kitchen staff to be seen. This was an opportunity for me to steal some food, as Mistress never left me much on her plate and sometimes nothing at all. So whenever I could take something from the kitchen I did. Today I pilfered a piece of cheddar cheese and ate it going back up the stairs. I made sure my mouth was empty before stepping back into Mistress Raven's room. Mistress took her tray of food and sat on the sofa to eat.

"You didn't do a very good job of cleaning the bathroom and you had all morning to do it, I'm unimpressed. You also completely forgot to mop the floor. Now, how am I to punish you?" Mistress said, tucking into her lunch of chicken and pasta. "In the second drawer of the dresser, you'll see a ping pong ball, fetch it for me.

I went to the drawer and sure enough, rolling around inside was a white ping pong ball. I took it over to Mistress. Mistress Raven looked at the ball in my hand and said:

Go over to the wall and place the ball between your nose and the wall and hold it there. So there is no cheating put your hands behind your back Do not drop the ball or else." Mistress said whilst stuffing her face with food. I did as I was told and put the ball on my nose and the wall and used as much pressure as I could to keep it there. I started to sweat, which exasperated the situation and the ball began to slip. I moved around a bit and managed to get the ball back under control, but because I was in an unusual position my back soon began to ache and I knew I would soon lose the ball. I suppose, I only lasted five minutes at best before the ping pong ball fell off my nose and bounced noisily along the floor and ironically settled at Mistress's feet.

"Oh dear, Oh dear, oh dear," you're in trouble now. I have finished eating you may take the tray down to the kitchen and when you return will sort you out for being disobedient."

I took Mistress's tray and left to go downstairs. There were very little in the way of scraps on her plate left for me, so I was pleased I took the piece of cheese earlier when I could, or I would be getting very hungry now. I was a bit apprehensive about returning to Mistress Raven as I knew she was going to punish me for losing the ping pong ball. Of course, I knew she expected me to drop the ball and it was all a part of the game she was playing.

I stepped back into the Mistress's room and gave a nice deep curtsey, hoping she might have forgotten her threat of punishment, but of course, as usual, I was wishful thinking.

"Come here and lie on the floor face down between the bed and the sofa. Now what you didn't know until now Daisy is, that I am very fond of rope work. Do you know what I mean by rope work?" She asked.

"You're going to tie me up?" I replied.

"Crudely put, but yes. I am going to tie you up, but trust me there is quite an art to it and some say it is a skill. Stay there face down whilst I ge some rope." Mistress said as she went off to rummage through a cupboard and she returned with some soft white rope."

Mistress spent ten minutes or so hog-tying me. It was very, very uncomfortable, my whole body ached. I started to beg and plead to be released.

"Release, release you," Mistress repeated incredulously. "I have only just tied you up you'll lie there on my floor hog-tied until I return for dinner." I continued to complain and my Mistress went off to the cupboard again and returned with the ball gag. When she put in my mouth and fastened it she said:

"That will stop you whinging like a baby, see you at dinner time, don't go anywhere", she added sarcastically. She knelt down and kissed me on the cheek and left the room. I was hog-tied for six hours, which felt more like sixty. I got cramps in every muscle in my body. No sooner had one muscle cramp relented another would start. I dearly wished Mistress had beaten me with the cane instead as a good canning would be lenient compared to this torture.

Mistress finally came back into the room and stepped over to me. I smelt her perfume as she leaned down to speak to me.

" There, there Daisy, are you getting stiff and sore, let's untie you, I think you have been punished enough." Mistress first removed the ball gag and then slowly loosens and removed the ropes. I turned over and sat up, and Mistress Raven began to massage my legs and arms.

“ A lady’s maid needs to learn how to cope with waiting, boredom and having nothing to do at times, for you, patience is a virtue. Now, go to the kitchen and get my dinner, and when you return and we have eaten I will have a little treat for you. Mistress noted the expression on my face. “A proper treat, nothing nasty, I promise, to make up for perhaps being a little cruel to you today,” she added

I brought Mistress’s dinner up from the kitchen for her. She ate ravenously and apologised for leaving me nothing on the plate. She suggested I ask the kitchen staff for some food when I took her dishes back to the kitchen. I did, but the kitchen staff refused to let me have any food as I was not on the staff list and I was Mistress Raven’s responsibility. When I returned I told Mistress what the kitchen staff said.

"Oh dear Daisy, we can't have you starving, can we? What can we do about this dreadful situation?" Mistress said with an insincere smile and sarcastic tone. Then her personality changed in an instant. "Take your piny and cap off." She ordered. She looked me up and down and said, "Yes you'll do. I don't suppose you have a coat do you Daisy, not much call for one when you're indoors all day?"

"No Mistress," I replied.

"Then I shall loan you one," Mistress replied going off to the wardrobe and returning with a light tan trench coat. "Put this one," she insisted, as she put on a coat herself. "You're very lucky my girl, I am still hungry too."

I followed Mistress downstairs and out of the house into the cold night air It felt so strange to be outside, I don't think I have been outside in the elements for over a year. It was also the first time I felt cold rise up my skirt another new sensation to enjoy. We walked a short distance to Mistress Raven's car. She used her fob to unlock the doors.

"Jump in," she said. After a short drive, we stopped at a Mac Donald's. "Do you want to eat in or out?" Mistress asked.

"Whichever you wish, "I replied.

"We'll eat in it will be a minor treat for you as you don't get out much," Mistress ordered a big mac and chips for both of us and a coffee for herself and coke for me. It was quite a treat it was the first full meal I had had in ages and I was out of the house a treat in itself.

"As I said Daisy, you're lucky I am still hungry or you would have had to go without until breakfast time and do not think this will become a habit. By the way, this isn't your treat, a treat awaits you when we get back to my room."

\fter the meal, I felt quite elated having a full ummy instead of hunger pains I usually felt. I vas so hungry I hadn't really absorbed I was out ınd about dressed in women's clothes for the irst time. It was only much later had I realised 10 one had taken any notice of me in the estaurant which was quite busy and full of oung women. My trench coat hid the maid's ıniform underneath from view. On the way ıome Mistress, Raven suggested a drink and we topped at a village pub about a mile from our ıouse. It was all very old worldly inside, lots of ıorse brasses and old oak beams. It was very leasant and I relaxed with Mistress as we both ıad a brandy each. However, Mistress wasn't oing to miss a chance to embarrass me and nsisted I went to the lady's toilet alone. I didn't vant to go but knew I had to and gingerly set off for the toilets. Mistress Raven watched me ike a hawk as she could see the lady's room from where she sat and saw me go in. Fortunately for me, the toilet was empty, but that didn't stop me from shaking like a leaf as I hadn't been in a public ladies' toilet before.

Back at the house Mistress and I returned to her room. My Mistress was quite chatty and much more approachable than usual, which also helped me to relax. I made another cup of coffee for us both and I joined Mistress on the sofa.

"I expect you're wondering what your treat is, would you like it now?" Mistress asked, turning on the sofa to face me full-on.

"Yes, please Mistress," I replied, not knowing what my treat was to be.

Mistress unbuttoned her blouse and reaching around her back, loosens her bra. Two voluptuous breasts were set free to bounce and settle on Mistress's chest. I looked at the wonderful specimens with awe and embarrassed myself by staring at them totally mesmerised.

"Go on, what are you waiting for?" Mistress asked. "Have a fondle and suck my nipples, this is your treat." I immediately began to fondle and suck and soon I had Mistress purring for more. I seemed to be sucking for an eternity, and then Mistress gently pushed me away, which was a relief as I needed to come up for air. She then undressed and lay on the bed, spread-eagled and said in an aroused husky voice:

"Now suck my pussy,"

I sucked away until Mistress came and let out a loud groan followed by two or three softer groans. Then she patted the bed at her side indicating she wanted me to come onto the bed and cuddle her.

"You're mine all mine," Mistress said, putting her arm around me then she drifted off to sleep.

I didn't mind being at her side was much better than sleeping in my dog basket, except a few hours, later Mistress pulled over the bedcovers and sent me back to the foot of the bed for the remainder of the night.

Chapter Nine

It wasn't long before I was back in Mistress's bad books. Not helped by my dropping Mistress's lunch tray down the stairs. It was a double compounded offence. Not only was I late bringing Mistress her lunch, but I had to stop and clear up the mess on the stairs and it was quite a mess with gravy splattered on the walls. I knew I was in deep trouble and in for a very hard time. Mistress saw the aftermath of the accident too, she heard the crash and came out of her room to look from the top of the stairs. The look she gave could have killed me.

When I finally returned with a fresh tray of food Mistress gave me one of her hard stares of disapproval and said as I put the tray of food down before her:

"I can see why you're looking so sheepish," Mistress said and you're quite right to think I am going to punish you severely. There is no excuse for dropping a tray it was the height of clumsiness and needs to be sorted. I won't have my maid embarrassing me in front of the other Masters and Mistresses. They will think I haven't trained you properly. What do you have to say for yourself?"

"I had wet hands and the tray slipped," I replied, knowing my excuse would not get me any mitigation at all.

"No excuse, go and stand in the corner until I decide what to do with you," Mistress ordered pointing to a vacant corner. A little while later

Mistress grabbed me by the arm and pushed me out of her room into the hallway. I was frog-marched downstairs and into the basement. I cringed as I knew I was in for a painful time as the basement was a dungeon and its sole purpose was to inflict pain on its victims.

"Strip down to your bra and panties." Mistress barked. "Fold your clothes up and put them on the table over there," she said pointing. When I was stripped I was tied to one of two pillars which held up an RSJ which kept the ceiling up. Then Mistress puts a ball gag in my mouth and attached a blindfold, then she rifled through some cardboard posters until she found one which said "beat me" and hung around my neck.

"You're now a whipping girl for all to use as they wish, I'll be back for you after dinner. Bye for now do enjoy yourself," she said, kissing me on the cheek and slapping my bottom with her hand as a parting gesture.

Then I was on my own at first it wasn’t too bad as I was on my own in the basement. I was hough, getting a bit cold as the basement was he coolest part of the house. It wasn’t long before I heard footsteps coming down the basement stairs. I heard two female voices:

“Look,” one of the voices said, “there is someone here already.” I heard the two women step over and read the sign on my back.

“She here to be whipped,” the second voice said.

“She has no marks on her, shall we be the first,” answered the first voice.

“Yes why not,” the second voice replied, “let's see what we can use.” The second voice came so close I could smell garlic on her breath.

“Why are you here, have you been a naughty maid?” She asked.

“I dropped a dinner tray down the stairs,” I replied.

“Oh yes,” I did hear about that, then you must be punished.

The ladies took turns beating me with a riding crop. Rhythmically one crop came down on one cheek, followed by the other on the other cheek until my bottom was a throbbing mass with me wriggling and withering in pain. Without another word they just left, leaving me on my own again. That was how the day went on, after a short while someone would appear and oblige me with a cane, whip or strap, sometimes on the buttocks or thighs or my back then go.

By the time my Mistress came to collect me, I was like tenderised meat. It didn’t stop her from having her session with me using a dressage whip. The pain was so much I just sank to my knees, but the punishment went on until Mistress was satisfied I had had enough.

"You may dress now," she said. "You may go to the kitchen and see if you can find something to eat as you have missed lunch and dinner today. You have ten minutes, then I expect you back in my room."

Mistress left after untying me, leaving me to dress and go off to the kitchen to find food. There was no kitchen staff to worry about they had long finished their work, so I had free rein to find whatever I could to eat. Most of the fridges were locked, but there were three meat pies on the hot plate. The pies were cold as the hot plate was long switched off, but I was so hungry they still tasted good. I ate two of the three pies before returning to Mistress's room.

On my arrival, I was told to strip again so Mistress could examine my welts. She positively loved running her fingers down the deepest welts.

“Um, you have had a good beating, haven’t you? I think you’ll have a better grip on the tray in the future when you’re coming up the stairs. Right, you can put on your nightie and go to bed, we have a long day tomorrow.”

“A long day?” I asked to repeat what Mistress had said.

“Yes, we are going out for the day,” Mistress replied.

“Both of us?” I asked.

“Yes, you too, so get to bed, I don’t want you tired tomorrow,” Mistress insisted.

“What will we be doing?” I asked.

“That’s enough Daisy unless you want some more fresh welts to go with the ones you have?”

As I didn’t fancy another beating I felt the conversation there, but I was very curious as to why I should be going along, I am usually left locked in the bathroom when Mistress is out. Why will she need me tomorrow?

Morning arrived and as usual, I got up, dressed and went down to the kitchen to get breakfast. The only difference this morning was I was still very sore from the beating yesterday. It was a mixture of stinging welts that broke the flesh and the dull throbbing pain of heavy bruising. When I returned with the breakfast, Mistress sat up in bed:

“While you were downstairs,” she said I have found an old dress you can wear today. I can’t have you going out dressed as you are it isn’t really suitable for outdoors. She pointed to a floral dress at the end of the bed. “Whilst I am eating you can go and change,” she said as she started her breakfast.

I went into the bathroom and put on the dress which was a long-sleeved midi dress. It was a predominantly yellow floral dress and I felt so different wearing it, as until now I was always dressed in a black maid’s uniform. When I returned to the bedroom Mistress looked up and agreed with me:

“Good lord,” you look so different. It is amazing what a simple dress can do to alter one image.”

“You can go and run my bath for me, whilst I finish my breakfast,” Mistress commanded. I did as asked and run the bath water. Mistress soon stepped in behind me totally in the nude and settled in the bath. I was about to leave, but she stopped me. “No, you may stay and wash my back for me.” She insisted.

began to soap Mistress back and then she said could now soap and bathe the rest of her taking pecial attention to her breasts. When I finished oaping her breasts I was told to wash between ıer legs before being dismissed. Finally, we vere both dressed to go out except I hadn't the oggiest idea of where we were going and Iistress despite my subtle questions, would not et on.

After quite a long car drive, we arrived at a ountry cottage deep in the countryside. We left he car and Mistress went ahead of me to knock on the door. The door opened and a young voman in her thirties greeted Mistress with a oig smile and a long hug.

"This must be Daisy," she said, looking back at ne.

“Yes,” Mistress said, “let me introduce you to my lady’s maid Daisy. Daisy this is Margaret a dear friend of mine.

“Well, don’t stand on the doorstep, do come inside where it is warm,” Margaret insisted.

We followed Margaret indoors and I immediately noted she had a pronounced limp. We were taken into the living room and Margaret left us to settle while she went off to make a brew for all of us. Mistress and I settled ourselves on the sofa while Margaret was in the kitchen. Mistress spoke in a soft voice so as not to be overheard.

Margaret has two children and she recently had a car accident and she isn’t coping very well,” Mistress said.

“I can see the house is clean but very untidy,” I replied and as I spoke it dawned on me why I was here.

"Yes, you have guessed," Mistress Raven said, noting the change of expression on my face as I realised why I was brought along. "You're here on loan to Margaret for a couple of days to get the house straight."

"But won't you need me?" I pleaded.

"I used to manage on my own before you became my lady's maid, I am sure I will manage for a week or so."

"I thought you said a couple of days?"

"I exaggerate," Mistress replied, stopping the conversation as Margaret returned with a tray. I jumped up to take the tray as she seemed a bit dodgy on her feet and I didn't fancy red hot tea in my lap.

"Once Daisy has had her cup of tea you can put her straight to work," Mistress said to Margaret.

“Oh, that will be such a help,” Margaret replied. “Can she do the laundry?” she asked as if I wasn’t there in person.

“Oh yes,” she is good at all domestic chores. However, she can be lazy so I have brought this for you,” Mistress said, retrieving a riding crop from her bag. “She works better with a slap or two with this now and again to help keep her motivated.” Margaret gratefully took the crop and thanked Mistress.

“So you had better watch out,” Margaret said waving the crop. “Can she start the laundry now?”

“Yes of course,” Mistress Raven replied. “Daisy, take your tea in the kitchen and sort out the washing.”

“You’ll see two baskets of whites and coloureds. There is also a tumble dryer and when the washing is finished and dried you can iron it all," Margaret said as if this was some sort of treat and I enjoyed doing housework.

I felt quite humiliated as I stepped into the kitchen and saw piles and piles of washing all waiting for my attention. In the meanwhile I could hear Margaret and Mistress chatting away, laughing and eating biscuits while I loaded the washing machine with soiled and dirty clothes.

Finally, Mistress Raven was shown to the front door, she stopped and stepped back into the kitchen entrance to speak to me.

"Margaret will look after you now. I expect good reports when I come back to collect you in a week or two," Mistress said before going out to her car. I noticed that a couple of days that Mistress spoke of has turned into a week which turned into a couple of weeks. Mistress Raven returned to the front door a moment or two later with a bag which she passed to Margaret and explained, that the clothes were for me, and then Mistress Raven was gone.

“You don’t need to worry about the children,” Margaret said, they are with their father for the summer holidays. There is just you and me and a house to keep clean.” Then she went back into the living room, leaving me with the laundry.

Chapter Ten

I don’t know which was worst Margaret or Mistress Raven as Margaret was also quite a taskmaster. I originally thought I was going to be in for a relatively easy time, but I was well mistaken about that. I was given the smallest bedroom in the house, which would normally be occupied by her youngest daughter. Not that the ize of the room mattered as I was hardly in here except to sleep. The moment I woke and dressed I was put to work. I grafted the whole day long only stopping for meals. No sooner had I finished one job than Margaret had another waiting for me.

The only saving grace was I could see the benefits of my work and the house was slowly transforming into a tidy, clean home. One day whilst I was vacuum cleaning and dusting there was a knock at the door. I crossed my fingers hoping it would be Mistress Raven coming to collect me, but to my horror, it was a man, a boyfriend of Margaret's.

He stopped in the doorway and hugged Margaret and then came into the house and as he made his way to the living room he spotted me.

"Who is that? He asked?"

"That's Daisy, she has helped me out with the housework for a couple of weeks whilst my leg gets better."

"What does she cost?" the man said, eying me up and down.

"Nothing," Margaret replied.

"Nothing?" The man repeated, "What do you mean nothing?"

"She is on loan to me from a friend, come and sit down," she insisted and I will explain.

I started to dust the skirting boards in the hall and could hear everything that was said in the living room. Margaret and her man had a bit of a fumble and grope then the conversation returned to me.

"You were going to explain why that woman is doing your housework for free?" the man asked

“Daisy,” Margaret shouted to me, “stop what you’re doing and make Peter and me a pot of tea.”

I went off to the kitchen and started a brew. All the while I was listening out to what was being said in the living room.

“I have a friend who employs Daisy and she has graciously loaned me Daisy to help me get the house straight and to take some of the load off me while I recover from my injury.”

“I see,” Peter replied, “and she does everything you ask of her?”

“Oh yes, she is quite an asset.

I now stepped into the living room and put the tray of tea down on the table and turned to go.

“Is she transgender?” Peter asked. “There is something not quite right about her.”

"Yes," Margaret replied, "she is, however, quite feminine and I am surprised you noticed."

"I've always fancied a transgender," Peter said whilst fondling Margaret.

"Well avert your eyes, you have me," Margaret said playfully. However, I cringed a bit as I wasn't so sure Peter was just being playful and I think he did have some designs on me. Despite his fondling and condoling with Margaret, he couldn't keep his eyes off me. So I moved away out of his sight, but close enough to still hear anything that was said between them.

"I have to go soon," Peter said, "I just nipped by whilst I had a few minutes to spare. Perhaps when I come again we can have a threesome with Daisy. Would you like that?"

"No way," Margaret said playfully punching Peter. "You'll have to make do with me alone."

"We'll see," said Peter standing up to put his coat on. "I'll see you sometime on Wednesday." Margaret saw Peter to the door and had one last long hug before letting him go.

I wasn't at all looking forward to Wednesday and didn't fancy a threesome. When Wednesday arrived, Peter called by in the evening. Much to my relief, I didn't come into the conversation at all. They just relaxed and cuddled on the living room sofa. I kept myself light on the ground and spent my time in the kitchen, but was close enough to the living room to hear anything that was said that might interest me.

I suppose two hours had passed when Peter was reminded of me. This wasn't helped by my dropping a salt cellar on the floor in the kitchen which brought me to the fore of Peter's mind, that someone else was in the house.

"Tell me more about Daisy?" Peter urged Margaret.

"What do you want to know? Margaret asked whilst kissing Peter's cheek.

"Will she do anything you ask of her?" Peter asked.

"Oh yes, you see she has a deep psychological need to be both submissive and obedient. She can't help it it is in her psyche and would see it as a failure not to please."

"That's interesting," Peter mused.

"I can beat her if I want. Daisy's Mistress gave me a riding crop to punish her if she is disobedient." Margaret said,

"Have you?" Peter asked.

"Have I what?" Margaret asked.

"Have you beaten her?" Peter asked again.

Oh no, that's not me. I could do anything like hat I am not cruel, besides, she does everything ask and works really hard. I would be lost vithout her whilst I am incapacitated."

Can I have some fun with her?" Peter asked.

No, you leave her alone." Margaret insisted.

Come on a little bit of fun it isn't going to hurt ıer," Peter pleaded.

What did you have in mind?" Margaret asked, just out of interest I'm not agreeing to nything." However, the change in Margaret's esponse was like a red flag to a bull.

Come on, let's go to the bedroom I have at east an hour before I have to leave," Peter said. Margaret assumed he had lost interest in Daisy nd wanted a bit of slap and tickle between the heets, so she willingly agreed and went into the bedroom and undressed while she thought Peter was in the bathroom.

Instead a few moments later, after Margaret had undressed and got under the covers Peter arrivec with a chair. Margaret rose from the covers and asked:

"What's the chair for?"

"You'll see," he said, disappearing for a second and returning with me blindfolded and then he tied me to the chair so I couldn't move.

"What are you doing?" Margaret asked in total confusion.

"I thought Daisy would like to hear what she is missing," Peter replied. I seemed, by my presence to add a bit of spice and risqué to the proceedings. I heard them romp in the bed and I couldn't avoid hearing all the sounds of rampan sex, culminating in loud groans and the strong smell of semen.

"That was the best sex in ages," Margaret agreed as she fought for breath.

"Yes, it is because Daisy is here listening to us, probably wishing it was her in the bed instead of you."

"I must admit it has made a difference to our sex, it has added a bit of excitement," Margaret agreed.

"I might have another treat for Daisy when I come next," Peter said wistfully.

"What is that," Margaret asked?"

"No that will spoil the surprise for both of you, you can wait and see," Peter said before dressing and announcing he had to go. I was untied and Peter left. Margaret and I then went to bed. Neither of us discussed what had happened, I think we were both too embarrassed.

What I didn't know was, that tonight was just a prelude to a tantalising introduction of much kinkier goings on in the future, which I wasn't sure I wanted to be involved in. I wasn't proven to be wrong a few days later Peter returned. The evening went quite normally until Margaret and Peter retired to the bedroom. I was in the kitchen and I heard Peter order Margaret to strip off and lie on the bed. Then he comes into the kitchen and blindfolded me again.

He guided me into the bedroom. Margaret was ordered to come to the edge of the bed and I was told to kneel and suck Margaret's pussy until she became aroused. Once Margaret was aroused. I was told to lie on the floor and Peter took over and it was another rock-rollicking success. Margaret and Peter had a simultaneous orgasmic experience and both let out a loud groan as they flopped over onto their backs to recover.

"Yes," Margaret agreed, "Daisy is adding a bit of spice to our relationship, this has been quite fun."

"It is called cuckolding," Peter said, "it is quite exquisite and probably very frustrating for Daisy. Maybe we can have a proper threesome next time, so Daisy can properly join in the fun."

All this was said as if I wasn't there I was never asked a thing. It was taken for granted that not only was I their domestic but I had somehow become their unwitting sex toy to add spice and amusement to their sex lives. They didn't care if I got anything from the arrangement or not, so long as I brought their sex to new heights.

Chapter Eleven

What is more, they hadn't reached the apex of their depravity. Whereas Margaret was once reluctant to involve me in their sex games, she was now of the opinion I did indeed enhance their sexual pleasure and encouraged Peter to dream up new ways to increase their sexual experience. Fortunately, because of Peter's work, he wasn't at the house more than once or twice a week. I consoled myself that soon Mistress Raven will want me back and collect me before things get too depraved. However, a few days later, Peter arrived one afternoon, which was unusual, a surprise, as he normally rolled up in the early evening or at night.

I made a pot of tea for them both and took it into the living room and left them to it. From the kitchen, I heard them fondling each other. I had hoped this was just a lightning visit, but as lways this was wishful thinking on my part. After an hour or so I was called into the living oom.

Margaret left to go upstairs and I was left with Peter on his own. I was told to go on my knees. have a surprise for you Daisy he said, inbuttoning his trousers. A moment later a emi-erect penis popped out into the fresh air.

Come on," Peter said, "you're a woman of the vorld, you know what I want you to do with his. As an encouragement, Peter lifted a ushion to expose a riding crop. "Take your hoice," he added looking at the implement. I lidn't fancy Peter beating me so I reluctantly noved a bit closer and began to suck his cock, which I could feel expanding in my mouth as I ucked.

Oh, I fancied you since I first set eyes on you," Peter purred under his breath as he became more aroused. “I always wondered what it would be like having a blow job from a transgender. I continued sucking and I could hear Margaret return to the room. She came over and stood briefly at my side so I could see whilst I sucked, she was wearing a strap-on with a huge black latex cock.

“I have come to join in the fun,” she said wistfully. She then went around to the back of me and lifted my skirt and pulled down both my tights and knickers together. Then I felt warm liquid being rubbed into the anus with her slender fingers. Then I felt the tip of the strap-on touch before she began to push it into me. This hurts a lot, but I continued to suck. Then Margaret began to thrust the strap-on in and out rhythmically to the beat of my sucking. We all rocked backwards and forwards in rhythmic unison, Margaret let out groans of delight and I could feel her move from side to side as she thrust in and out. After several minutes of this finally, both Peter and Margaret orgasmed almost at the same time.

Margaret rolled off of me and shouted almost at the top of her voice:

"Oh my god no."

Then Peter pushed me away and also looked stunned. I was shocked too, as I couldn't imagine what had brought on this sudden response. I then looked around and I could instantly see why. Mistress Raven stood at the living room door with her arms on her hips looking incredibly angry. I had never seen her look so angry.

"If you're going to have sex, especially with my maid, I suggest, in the future locking the front door. I knocked several times and then I noticed the door was ajar, so I let myself in. This was not what I expected to see. Daisy," she said, looking at me, “go to the bathroom clean yourself up, straighten your clothes and come back with your bags packed,” Mistress ordered. I immediately left for the bathroom, as I went I could hear Mistress Raven admonish Margaret and her boyfriend.

“You have betrayed my trust,” she announced. “I loaned Daisy to you to help with domestic work not to enhance your sex lives. You won’t be hearing from me again our friendship is over. Daisy, are you ready to go, yet,” Mistress Raven shouted up the stairs.

“Nearly,” I shouted down.

“Hurry up, the sooner we get out of this house the better,” Mistress said waiting at the bottom of the stairs for me. I grabbed my bag and came down the stairs to join Mistress.

“Have you everything?” She asked.

“Yes Mistress,” I replied,

“If you are sure then let go, to the car and get out of here,” Mistress urged, pushing me out of the front door. Once in Mistress’s car, I could tell from her silence and driving she was quite a bit upset. I thought it was down to me, to be the first to speak.

“I am sorry,” I said, somewhat inadequately. “I didn’t have a choice, You told me to obey Margaret implicitly. Besides, what could I do to stop them, I had no way to reach or call you.”

“It is of no interest what they were doing to you,” Mistress said breaking the silence. I don’t care if you found it enjoyable or distasteful you’re a slave of no value at all, your feelings are the last thing on my mind.”

“Oh,” I replied, feeling a bit dejected.

"The reason I am angry is not that you have been violated against your will, but the fact I had loaned you for domestic work only, Margaret had betrayed that trust given to her, that's why I am furious. But get this in your head Daisy I didn't save you from Margaret and her boyfriend for your sake, I didn't see why they should enjoy you sexually when you belong to me. When we get home I shall show you how important you are."

As much as Mistress tried to demonstrate how lowly and completely unimportant I am, I could help but think a fair amount of her anger was directed at me, regardless of what she said. I think this was born out when we returned home and I was back to performing lady's maid duties. That night after I had brought Mistress Ravan up her dinner, she told me to strip off and lie on my back in the empty Jacuzzi. I was in the bath naked, whilst Mistress finished her dinner.

began to shiver a bit as the enamel of the acuzzi was cold to the touch. A short while ater she returned, she too was now completely ıaked.

;he also had in her hand a fluted glass. She traddled herself over me and peed into the ;lass.

'This is for you, drink it all, there's a good girl, nd show Mistress how obedient you can be. Come on then take the glass." I took the glass nd drank the contents and immediately began o choke and splutter. The taste of the drink was lisgusting.

I apologise, forgive me, I should have brought ome ice for your drink," Mistress Raven said arcastically. "Stay where you are, we haven't inished. I want to show you how important you ire to me. Mistress stood and emptied her bladder on me, moving forward and backwards so I was evenly covered in a stream of pee.

"You're going to be my urinal for the rest of the evening, you'll stay in the Jacuzzi wallowing in my pee until I next need to go," with those words she left the bathroom. Mistress returned another three times that evening and peed over me including my face. Finally, I was allowed to wash and dry myself. I returned to the bedroom in a dressing gown to find Mistress was already in bed.

"You can take the dinner plates down to the kitchen in the morning when you go down to ge breakfast. Now come here and kneel beside my bed. Your ordeal isn't over yet, I have decided to be stricter with you from now on. Do you understand?" Mistress asked.

"Yes Mistress," I replied, knowing she was indeed very angry with me and I was going to pay for my goings on with Margaret and her boyfriend, even though it was entirely out of my control.

“Some slaves are taught slave positions. There are around fourteen of them, but we will concentrate on the five most commonly used. Let’s start tonight with the first one. From under the covers she produced a riding crop. “An occasional flick with this will help you learn. Now take your dressing gown off and come and kneel again here close to my side.” When I returned naked Mistress parted my legs with the tip of the crop.

“Now kneel on your ankles and put your hands behind your back and tilt your chin down, this is the Number One position, the position you’ll use the most. Every night before you go to bed, you’ll come to my side and take this position whilst you await further instructions.”

“Are you still angry with me?” I asked Mistress.

“I have gone to great lengths to explain to you. You mean nothing to me, you have no rights, not a single one, and you’re just property, a chattel, a possession. You’re useful to me, but far from indispensable. Hundreds of submissives would beg to be you. Now you may go to bed and think yourself lucky.”

The End.

Check out my other books:

The Chronicles of a Male Slave.

A real-life account of a consensual slave. The book follows the life of an individual who comes to terms with his submissive side and his search for a Mistress and his subsequent

experiences as a consensual slave.
This book gives a real insight into the B.D.S.M., lifestyle and what it is like to be a real slave to a lifestyle Mistress.

Mistress Margaret.

This is the story of young teenage Brenden, who is finding out about his sexuality when he meets older Mistress Margaret a nonprofessional dominatrix. Mistress Margaret takes Brenden's hand and shows him the mysterious, erotic world of BDSM and all it has to offer.

The Week That Changed My Life.

A tale about a young girl discovering her sexuality with an older, more mature dominant man whilst on a week's holiday by the sea. She was introduced into a world of BDSM that would change her outlook on life forever.

The Temple of Gor.

Hidden in the wilds of Scotland is The Temple of Gor, a secret BDSM society. In the Temple, you will find Masters and their female slaves living in a shared commune. The community is based on the Gorean subculture depicted in a fictional novel by John Norman and has taken a step too far and turned into a macabre reality. Stella a young girl from England, stumbles on the commune and is captured and turned into a Kajira slave girl until she finds a way to escape her captors.

Becoming a Sissy Maid.

This is a true story of one person's quest to become a sissy maid for a dominant couple. The story outlines the correspondence between the Master, Mistress, and sissy maid, which leads up to their first and second real-time meeting.

It is a fascinating tale and is a true, honest and accurate account, only the names and places ave been changed to protect the individuals nvolved. It is a must-be-read book by anyone nto BDSM and will give an interesting insight or anyone wishing to become, in the future a eal-time sissy maid.

Meet Maisy The Sissy Maid.

This story is about Maisy a sissy maid and her ife. The story takes Maisy through all the arious stages a sissy has to make take to find er true submissive and feminine self. It is a ong and arduous road and many transitions efore Maisy finds true happiness as a lady's naid for her Mistress.

Beginner's Guide For The Serious Sissy

So you want to be a woman and dress and ehave like a sissy? You accept you cannot ompete with most men and now want to try omething new and different. This guide will elp you along the way and walk the potential sissy through the advantages and pitfalls of living as a submissive woman.

Becoming a serious sissy requires making changes that are both physical and mental. This will involve learning to cross-dress, leg-crossing, sit, stand, bend hair removal, wear makeup, use cosmetics, and sit down to pee. You'll learn feminine mannerisms such as stepping daintily, arching your spine, swishing your hips, and adopting a feminine voice. You'l understand more about hormone treatment and herbal supplements.

There is advice and tips on going out in public for the first time and coming out of the closet to friends, colleagues, and family. The guide will give help you to slowly lose your masculine identity and replace it with a softer gentle feminine one.

A Collaring For A Sissy.

Collaring ceremonies are taken very seriously by the BDSM community and are tantamount to a traditional wedding. Lots of thought and planning go into such an event and can take many forms.

Mistress Anastasia's sissy maid Paula has just completed her six months probation and has earned her collar. This is a story about Paula's service and her subsequent collaring ceremony.

The Secret Society.

Rene Glock is a freelance journalist looking for a national scoop and attempts to uncover and expose a Secret Society of Goreans which have set up residence in an old nightclub. However, as he delves into the secret world he finds he has an interest in BDSM and questions his moral right to interfere in what goes on in the Gorean Lodge.

The Good Master and Mistress Guide.

If you want to become a good Dominant and practice BDSM in a safe and considerate way, then this guide is for you.

It is written by a submission that has had many dominants male and female over the years and knows what goes into becoming a good dominant and the mistakes some dominants make.

The book is not aimed to teach, but to make the fledgling dominant understand what is going on in the dominant-submissive dynamic, so they can understand their charges better and become better dominants.

My Transgender Journey

This is a true story with some minor alterations to protect people's identities. It is a tale about my own journey into transgender and my eventual decision to come out.

It is hoped that others can share my experiences, relate to them and perhaps take comfort from some of them.

The book has some BDSM content but is only used to put my story into context, it's about my experiences, trials and tribulations of coming out and living as a female full-time.

I hope you enjoy my little story.

Cinders

Cinders is the BDSM version of Cinderella. It is a story where an orphaned Tommy is sent to be brought up by his aunt and two very beautiful sisters.

The sisters were cruel and taunting and dressed Tommy up like a Barbie Doll. One day Tommy was caught with auntie's bra and knickers and as a punishment, he was a feminist and turned into Nancy the maid. Poor Nancy is consigned to a life of drudgery and final acceptance of life as a menial skivvy.

This story doesn't have a glass slipper or a prince, but Nancy is given a present of some new rubber gloves and a bottle of bleach. There is no happy ending or is there, you decide.

At The Races

Ryan is a hotel night porter and is at a crossroads in his life. He feels his talents are being wasted in a job with no future. Through a friend, he is offered a managerial position on a farm in Catalonia, Spain. He decides to take the post but has no idea what sort of farm he is going to work at.

Only on the flight out to Spain does Ryan realise that there is more to the farm than rearing chickens and growing vegetables. Later e learns the main event of the year is The Derby and there isn't a horse in sight.

Nearly Married A Dominatrix

This is a true story that I have changed a little bit to protect people from identification. It's a story about a man's constant struggle and fights against his deep-rooted need to be submissive and a woman who conversely, is very comfortable with her dominance and heavily into the BDSM lifestyle.

They meet and get along very well indeed until Mistress Fiona announces she wants to become a professional dominatrix. Rex, the submissive boyfriend goes along with his Mistress's plans, reluctantly, but as time goes by there are more and more complications heaped on the relationship until it snaps.

Be careful what you ask for

There is an old English adage: Be careful abou what you ask for; it may come true.

This is a story about a BDSM fantasy that has gone badly wrong.

Fantasy is simply a fantasy and we all have them regardless of our sexuality. Fantasies are quite harmless until we choose to act them out for real and when do act out our fantasies the line between fantasy and reality can become very blurred. This is a tale about one person's fantasy that becomes all too real for comfort.

Petticoat Lane.

A slightly effeminate young boy is taken unde the wings of his school teacher. She becomes his guardian and trains him to become a servan girl to serve her for the rest of his life.

An unexpected incident happens and Lucy the maid has an opportunity to escape her life of drudgery and servitude, but does she take the opportunity or does she stay with her Mistress?

I Became a Kajira slave girl.

A Gorean scout Simon, who is looking for new talent kidnaps Emma a PhD student on sabbatical with her friend Zoey in Spain. Emma is half-drugged and sent across the ocean to the United States and ends up in the clandestine City of Gor in the Mojave desert sixty miles from civilization.

Here there is no law women are mere objects for the pleasure of men. Emma becomes a Kajira a female slave whose sole purpose in life is to please her master or be beaten tortured or killed.

Two years into Emma's servitude and she meets Simon again. Simon is consumed with guilt when he sees what Emma has been reduced to, a beaten, downtrodden and abused slave. He vows to free her from her servitude, But how they are in one of the biggest deserts in the world and sixty miles from anywhere?

Training My First Sissy Maid.

A young single mother with a part-time job, two teenage children, and up to her knees in housework is at the end of her tether and finding it harder and harder to cope.

Then reading one of her daughter's kinky magazines she found in her bedroom whilst tidying, read an article about sissy maids who are willing to work without pay just for discipline, control and structure to their lives. Excited about the prospect she decides a maid is an answer to her domestic problems.

She sets about finding a sissy to come and do her housework and be trained and moulded into becoming her loyal obedient sissy maid. On the journey she discovers she is a natural dominant and training her maid becomes a highly erotic and fulfilling experience.

A Week with Mistress Sadistic.

Susan a young female reporter in her thirties wants to know more about B.D.S.M for a future article in her magazine. She arranged to spend a week with Mistress Sadistic and watch how a professional dominatrix works.

After an eye-opening week of watching Mistress Sadistic deal with her many and varied clients, Mistress Sadistic wonders if Susan might be submissive and puts her to the text to make Susan her personal slave.

Lady Frobisher and her maid Alice.

This is a gripping tale of BDSM in Victorian England. It is a story about the lives of Lady Frobisher and her hapless maid Alice. It is a tale of lesbianism and sexual sadism with a twist at the end.

If you enjoy reading BDSM literature you'll love this as it has everything woven into an interesting tale of two people's lives at the top end of society.

K9

This is a tale that explores an area of B.D.S.M where a Mistress or Master desires a human dog (submissive) to train and treat as a real dog in every respect. Mistress Cruella is one such Mistress who takes on a young male submissive as her human dog and she takes the role of Mistress and her dog very seriously indeed.

Ryan soon becomes Max the Poodle and he struggles with his new role as a pooch but learns to be an obedient dog to please his Mistress. Max soon discovers there is far more to being a dog than meets the eye.

3ridget Monroe's Finishing School for ;issies.

3ridget and her husband are both dominant and ıave their own sissy maid Isabel to help them vith housework. One day when the couple were n holiday in Kent, Bridget discovered an empty ıanor house in need of extensive repairs. On nquires, she decides to buy the manor but soon ealises that to pay for the mortgage and repair osts the manor house will need to be run as a usiness.

3ridget used willing slaves in the B.D.S.M., ommunity to help repair and renovate the ıanor house and later it was decided on advice rom friends to open the manor house as a inishing school for sissies. A business had been orn and later other B.D.S.M., activities were dded to the core business, which included orture rooms and a medieval dungeon. Once a month an open day was held at the academy held pony races, yard sales and schoolboy classes. This also included K9 dog shows, beer tents and other amenities intending to satisfy th whole B.D.S.M., community.

Just when the business was taking off and in profit disaster struck. Society wasn't ready for Bridget Monroe's Finishing School for Sissies and Bridget was forced to close.

Printed in Great Britain
by Amazon